Bed Bugs

by Bobby Lynn Maslen
pictures by John R. Maslen

Scholastic Inc.
New York • Toronto • London • Auckland • Sydney • Mexico City • New Delhi • Hong Kong • Buenos Aires

Available Bob Books®:

Set 1: Beginning Readers — With consistent new sounds added gradually, your new reader is gently introduced to all the letters of the alphabet. They can soon say, "I read the whole book!®"

Set 2: Advancing Beginners — The use of three-letter words and consistent vowel sounds in slightly longer stories build skill and confidence.

Set 3: Word Families — Consonant blends, endings and a few sight words advance reading skills while the use of word families keep reading manageable.

Set 4: Complex Words — Longer books and complex words engage young readers as proficiency advances.

Set 5: Long Vowels — Silent *e* and other vowel blends build young readers' vocabulary and aptitude.

Bob Books® Collections:

Collection 1 — Includes Set 1: Beginning Readers and part of Set 2: Advancing Beginners

Collection 2 — Includes part of Set 2: Advancing Beginners and Set 3: Word Families

Collection 3 — Includes Set 4: Complex Words and Set 5: Long Vowels

Ask for Bob Books at your local bookstore, or visit www.bobbooks.com.

ISBN 0-545-02695-4

6 5 4 3 2   10 11/0

Printed in China   68
This edition first printing, September 2007

The clock struck ten.

Meg and Fred were sent to bed.

But Fred and Meg jumped on the bed.

Fred jumped up.

Meg jumped down.

Fred felt the bed bend.
Meg felt the bed bump.

Mama said, "Fred, don't jump on that bed."

Papa said, "Meg fell on her head."

Papa was upset.
Mama was upset.

Mama said, "Get your rest."
Papa said, "Hush all that fuss."

But Meg and Fred jumped
and the big bed fell, KER-PLUNK!

And that was the end of jumping on the bed. "Good night, Meg. Good night, Fred."

The End

List of 42 words in <u>Bed Bugs</u>

<u>Short Vowels</u>

<u>a</u>	<u>e</u>	<u>i</u>	<u>o</u>	<u>u</u>	<u>sight</u>	
and	ten	big	on	up	to	Papa
that	bed		clock	upset	the	said
	get			but	was	head
	end			jump	all	don't
	fell			bump	her	down
	Meg			fuss	ker-plunk	of
	Fred			hush	were	
	felt			plunk	your	
	sent			struck	good night	
	bend			bugs	Mama	
	rest					

96 total words in *Bed Bugs*